PLAY SCHOOL STORIES

Since its start in 1964, *Play School*, BBC Television's daily programme for the under fives, has aimed at enriching the experience of the child, and providing a foundation for later formal learning.

This new collection of stories from *Play School* has been carefully selected to mirror the variety and above all the fun of the programmes, and in addition to appealing to those caring for the under fives, provides material for those children starting to read for themselves.

PLAY SCHOOL STORIES

Stories and rhymes from the
BBC television programme
Play School

Illustrated by Tony Morris

BBC/KNIGHT BOOKS.

Copyright © British Broadcasting Corporation
and the Contributors 1982

First published 1982 by British Broadcasting
Corporation/Knight Books

British Library C.I.P.

Play School stories
   1. Children's stories, English
   I. British Broadcasting Corporation.
   823'.01'089282 [J]   PZ5

   ISBN 0-340-28086-7
      (0-563-20052-9 BBC)

Printed and bound in Great Britain for the British
Broadcasting Corporation, 35 Marylebone High Street,
London W1M 4AA and Hodder and Stoughton
Paperbacks, a division of Hodder and Stoughton Ltd,
Mill Road, Dunton Green, Sevenoaks, Kent (Editorial
Office: 47 Bedford Square, London, WC1 3DP) by
Cox & Wyman Ltd, Reading, Berks.
Photoset by Rowland Phototypesetting Ltd,
Bury St Edmunds, Suffolk.

Contents

Can you guess what animal this is?
> Four stiff-standers,
> Four dilly-danders,
> Two lookers,
> Two crookers,
> And a wig-wag.

It's a Cow!

The Cow Jumped
Over the Moon

AVRIL PRICE

Once there was a cow called Buttercup. She lived on a farm with nineteen other cows and, most of the time, Buttercup was very happy. Most of the time, that is, apart from the afternoons. That was the time when all the cows would lie in the sun to chew their cuds and Buttercup felt just a little bit bored.

"Oh dear," thought Buttercup one afternoon. "There must be more to do than this!" And with that, the farmer's young daughter looked over the gate.

"Hello cows," she said, then she started to sing:

7

Hey diddle diddle
The cat and the fiddle
The cow jumped over the moon.
The little dog laughed to see such sport
And the dish ran away with the spoon.

Then she waved at the cows and skipped off down the lane.

Buttercup was very excited. A cow jumping over the moon! That gave her an idea.

"Perhaps," thought Buttercup, "if I practise jumping a lot, I may be able to jump over the moon just like the cow in the song."

So she looked around for something to jump over. That hedge would do for a start! She stood well back to take a long run: one . . . two . . . three . . . *hup*! Over the hedge she went, straight into the next field.

"That was easy!" she said. "I'll try something a bit higher." She saw a fence on the other side of the field so she ran towards it. One . . . two . . . three . . . *hup*! Over the fence she went, straight into the next field.

Unfortunately for Buttercup, this field was a hayfield and Tom, the farmer's son, was just about to climb on to his tractor to start baling the hay. He had such a fright when Buttercup landed next to him that he left his tractor and led her back to the farm.

"You come back to your shed, Buttercup," he said, "and see that you stay there till milking time!"

Buttercup couldn't practise any more jumping that afternoon because she had to stand very still in her stall. But as soon as milking was over and she was let out again she trotted down the lane, into the field and jumped straight out again, over the hedge.

The cowman couldn't think what had got into Buttercup, who had never been any trouble before. So he led Buttercup back to her field and shut the gate. "In you go and stay there," he said.

Buttercup decided she had better stay put for the rest of the day. She could hardly wait for it to be dark to see if the moon was up.

Suddenly, there it was, big and yellow over the treetops.

At once Buttercup ran towards it and jumped as high as she could. But of course, the moon was still in front of her. Then she tried jumping from one side to the other, but the moon remained in front of her. She didn't give up though, and kept on jumping as hard as she could to try and jump over the moon. She carried on for so long that she made herself thirsty. She'd just have to have a drink of water. So off she went to the pond in the corner of the field.

Then she saw something very strange! There, in the middle of the pond, was a moon, just like the one up in the sky. And with no effort at all, Buttercup jumped right over it. She was so excited that she jumped over it again and again. And from that day till this she's never jumped out of her field again. But every evening after milking, Buttercup runs straight to the pond and starts jumping over the moon.

Have you ever been on a bus? This is the tale of Maisie Blundell's bus which drove off in search of the sun.

Maisie Blundell's Bus

JUDY WHITFIELD

Here comes Maisie Blundell's bus
Not much noise and not much fuss,
Driving through the snow in search of the sun
Wheels going round, engine going brrrm!

The motorway looks smooth and flat
Maisie drives fast and holds on to her hat.
Then bump and clunk and up and down . . .
Maisie's bus hits rocky ground,
But the wheels go round and the engine goes brrrm
As the Blundell bus trundles in search of the sun.
It goes over a viaduct arching and wide,
Then into a tunnel that's pitch dark inside,
But the wheels go round and the engine goes brrrm
As the Blundell bus trundles in search of the sun.

And through a town all smoky and gritty
With the bustle and hustle and hum of a city,
Then into the country, just fields and trees
And hills and birds, and flowers and peace.
And the wheels go round and the engine goes brrrm
As the Blundell bus trundles in search of the sun.

And into a storm of wind and showers,
That pour on the bus for hours and hours,
And the wheels go round and the engine goes brrrm
As the Blundell bus trundles in search of the sun.

But – here is the sun and the sand and the sea,
Maisie has found where she wanted to be.
The wheels went round and the engine went brrrm!
Goodbye to the cold – hello to the sun!

*   *   *

What colour are the buses where you
live? Next time you're waiting at a
bus stop, try counting how many cars
pass before your bus arrives. What
number is your bus?

In Northern Ireland there is an unusual rock formation known as the
Giant's Causeway. This is one of the
traditional stories about how it was
formed.

The Giant's Causeway

Once upon a time there lived in Ireland a
giant called Finn McCool.

He was so tall that his head touched the
clouds.

He was so big that when he breathed it
made a rushing wind up and down the glen.

When he laughed it sounded like thunder
over Knockmany hill.

His arms and legs were the size of oak trees,
and when he walked round the countryside
he left footprints the size of cars.

He was enormous . . . a real giant!

He was a good giant – he was always care-
ful not to hurt the people who lived nearby.
He enjoyed his life of lazy days walking by the
sea and nights spent counting the stars.

However, across the sea in Scotland there
lived another giant. A proud giant who
wanted everyone to know that he was the
biggest giant in the world. When he heard

how big Finn McCool was he decided he would fight him to prove that he was bigger and stronger. But Finn McCool lived in Ireland and the Scottish giant lived in Scotland. And the Irish sea flowed in between.

They decided to build a bridge across the sea so they could meet and fight. Finn McCool and the Scottish giant each took the most enormous boulders they could find and threw them into the sea, one after the other.

So there were broad roads of boulders reaching out into the sea from Ireland and from Scotland. And at last the roads met in the middle and formed a giants' causeway across the Irish sea.

That night Finn sat watching the Scottish giant putting the last rock in to the causeway. He was worried – he knew they'd have to fight the next day and the Scottish giant was enormous, even bigger than himself. Finn would be surely beaten. He had to think of something.

Slowly an idea came to him . . .

Early next morning, Finn did a very strange thing. Instead of going out to meet the Scottish giant he put on a baby's bonnet and squeezed into the baby's cradle standing in the corner of the room. He covered himself with a fluffy blanket and began to suck his thumb.

Soon his house began to tremble as the Scottish giant tramped up from the shore. When he arrived at Finn's house he flung open the door.

"Where's Finn McCool?" he shouted . . . but there was no reply. The only living creature was the biggest baby he'd ever seen, lying in a cradle in the corner of the room.

"Och no!" cried the Scottish giant. "Thank goodness Finn McCool's not in! If that is the size of his baby son, Finn must be enormous!"

With a leap and a bound and a squeal the Scottish giant ran all the way back to Scotland. And as he went he pulled up the rocks and stones from the causeway and threw them into the sea.

Finn McCool crept out of the cradle and laughed and laughed. For he knew that the Scottish giant would never bother him again.

*   *   *

What do you think the Scottish giant's name was?

Did you ever see Giant Frodge-dobbulum,
With his double great-toe and his double
  great-thumb?

Did you ever hear Giant Frodge-dobbulum
Saying Fa-fe-fi *and* fo-faw-fum?

He shakes the earth as he walks along,
As deep as the sea, as far as Hong-Kong!

He is a giant and no mistake,
With teeth like the prongs of a garden rake.

This story could be told with simple props if you like – a walking stick, old clothes, a picture etc.

Kindhearted Jack

JEAN WATSON

Jack was a kind man. Every Saturday morning, he would drive to town in his little black car to do his shopping. On the way he would stop at a row of bungalows where some old people lived to find out whether they wanted him to do any little jobs for them. If they did, they would leave notes for him outside their back doors.

One Saturday morning, Jack's car wouldn't start. "Oh dear, I shall have to walk," he thought. "Good thing it's a nice day. Hope the old folk won't *all* want jobs done today!"

He set off, whistling cheerfully.

When he reached the first bungalow, he went round to the back and saw a walking stick propped against the door with a note stuck to it. The note said:

Dear Jack, please could you drop this stick into Mr Jones' house in the High Street? He left it behind the other day. Thank you so much. Ezra Smith.

"Well, carrying a walking stick won't be any trouble," thought Jack, picking it up and walking off towards the second bungalow.

Round the back was a saucepan and another note. The note said:

Dear Jack, would you be kind enough to take this saucepan to the shop to be mended. The handle's loose. Thank you. Enid Pearce.

"I can manage that, all right," thought Jack, picking up the saucepan and walking off towards the third bungalow.

There he found a jacket hanging from the

door handle with another note pinned to it. The note said:

I should be grateful if you would drop this jacket in to the cleaners. Thank you. John Brown.

"No problem," thought Jack, putting the jacket over his arm and walking towards the fourth bungalow, "but I hope there won't be too many more things to carry."

But there were!

At the fourth bungalow were three plastic jugs which Mrs Raynor wanted to be delivered to Mrs Moore who would need them for a party.

At the fifth bungalow there was a picture which Mr Peabody wanted Jack to take to the picture shop.

At the sixth bungalow, there was a cushion which Mr Timmins wanted re-covered.

At the seventh bungalow were some spectacle frames with a note which said:

Dear Jack, please could you ask the optician to make these into dark glasses for my summer holiday? Thank you. Maureen Elliott.

At the eighth bungalow was a big parcel tied with ribbon to be given to the butcher because it was his birthday and he was always very helpful to the old people.

Poor Jack! By this time his arms were piled

high with all the things he had collected. In fact, because he couldn't see where he was going, he tripped over a bumpy bit of the pavement and dropped everything.

"Oh dear," thought Jack, looking round at the untidy pile. "What am I going to do? I don't want to disappoint the old folk, but how am I going to manage? It's not that the things are heavy – just *awkward*!"

Jack stood on the pavement and thought. Then he had a good idea, and a big smile spread across his face. First he picked up the jacket and put it on, but before he buttoned it up, he tucked the cushion safely inside it. Then he put the saucepan on his head and

the spectacle frames on his nose.

"Now," he thought, "that leaves the walking stick, three plastic jugs, the picture and the parcel." With a chuckle, he picked up the walking stick and threaded it *through* the handles of the plastic jugs, *under* the string behind the pictures, and *in and out* of the ribbon round the parcel. Then he put the walking stick carefully over his shoulder with the jugs and picture hanging from one end and the parcel from the other!

Off he went, carrying everything quite easily, and smiling happily. And everyone he met smiled back at Kindhearted Jack.

Have you ever looked up in the sky and not been quite sure what you could see? A bird? A plane? A kite? Listen to what people thought they could see in this story of

The New Blue Umbrella

CHRISTOPHER WALKER

Mrs Brown had a new, blue umbrella. Blue was her favourite colour and this umbrella was the prettiest blue she had ever seen. She had ordered it specially from the shop and there was a little label tied on the handle, which read: MRS BROWN, 2 PARK ROAD. PAID.

She decided to take it out shopping with her. "It looks like rain," she said.

She carried the umbrella with her down the High Street and in and out of the shops. When she was coming out of the butcher's, a strong wind started to blow and Mrs Brown felt some drops of rain. She put down her basket and put up her new, blue umbrella. As soon as she had put it up, a really strong gust of wind came and snatched the umbrella out of her hand.

"Oh no!" cried Mrs Brown as the umbrella

flew up into the air. "The first time I've taken it out too!"

The blue umbrella sailed over the shops and out of sight. Mrs Brown sadly picked up her basket and walked off without her umbrella.

Some children were in the playground of the school. "Look, look!" they said. "A blue kite!"

Their teacher came to see what they were pointing at. But the wind had blown the blue umbrella somewhere else. "There's nothing there," said the teacher.

The wind continued to play with the umbrella, turning it over and over and over. It was flying upside down when it passed over the house of old Mr Gryce. He was in his garden.

"A flying saucer! A flying saucer!" he shouted to his wife. "Where's my telescope?"

By the time Mr Gryce had found his telescope, the wind had carried the umbrella away. "There's nothing there," said Mrs Gryce.

Miss Hodge was dozing by her window. She opened her eyes and saw something large and blue fly past. "A butterfly! A butterfly!" Her sister had been sleeping in the next chair. She sat up and looked out. "There's nothing there," said Miss Hodge's sister.

At last the wind stopped blowing so hard and the new, blue umbrella came gently down to land in a corner of the park. A policeman found it on the ground. He picked it up and read the label on the handle: MRS BROWN, 2 PARK ROAD. PAID.

"I know where Park Road is," he said. "I'll take it round on my way home."

There was nobody in at Mrs Brown's house so the policeman left the blue umbrella hanging on the gate.

As Mrs Brown came down the road, carrying her heavy shopping basket, she could see something blue outside her house. When she got there she saw it was her new, blue umbrella – the umbrella she had lost. "Well I never!" said Mrs Brown. "It's found its own way home!"

And she picked up her basket and the new, blue umbrella and went into the house.

*   *   *

Do you know your address? And the name of your town or village?

It's raining, it's pouring,
The old man's snoring
He went to bed with a cold in his head
And couldn't get up in the morning!

Who is the tallest person you know?

The Tall Thin Man

URSULA DANIELS

Jim lived in a house with a garden. At the end of the garden was a very high wall. It was so high that Jim could not see over it, but he would often listen to sounds of the traffic passing on the road behind the wall.

Sometimes he could hear a motorbike.

Sometimes he could hear a police siren.

Sometimes he could just see the top of a big red double-decker bus.

He could hear the people chatting as they walked to the station in one direction, or to the shops in the other direction.

Sometimes he could hear the clip-clopping of a horse passing by.

Once he heard a dog barking at his cat sitting on the top of the wall. The cat could see everything, but Jim could only see the sky, and the roofs of the buildings across the road.

One day there was a lot of commotion in the street on the other side of the wall. There was music playing, people laughing, and the noises of big lorries driving down the street in the direction of the shops. What was happening?

Then a man in a funny hat with a daisy on it walked past.

That's strange, thought Jim. That's very strange, because all I can ever see over this wall is the tops of big red double-decker buses.

Jim ran indoors to find his father. "Come and see a man as tall as a red double-decker bus!" he shouted.

But when they both went out into the garden again there was nothing there. Jim was upset. "There really *was* a man in a funny hat with a daisy on it. He walked along there going towards the shops."

Jim's father could not see anything. "Come along," he said, "let's go to the shops and get that cat food we need, and we'll keep our eyes open for hats with daisies."

So they went back through the house, out on to the pavement at the front of the house and walked towards the shops.

As they walked along they heard music, and the nearer they came to the shops, the louder the music became.

"That's the tall man's music!" said Jim. "That's the music I heard when the tall man walked by behind the wall."

As they turned the last corner they saw, in the park by the shops, a band, and tents and a clown . . . and walking along the pavement was a man, a very tall man.

"Well, look at that!" Jim's father exclaimed. "He *is* as tall as a double-decker bus!"

"What long stripy trousers," said Jim, "and look, he *has* got a hat with a daisy. But . . . he's got no shoes." Then he whispered:

"He hasn't even got any feet, just bits of wood! Has he really got two wooden legs?"

"Yes," laughed his father, "two wooden legs called stilts. He's walking on stilts, the long trousers are hiding them."

"If we went to the circus," Jim said, "we could have a proper look. Let's go."

The next day that's just what they did – and the tall man on stilts with the hat with the daisy on top was leading the circus parade.

*   *   *

32

It's hard to balance on stilts – but you make yourself as tall as you can by standing on tip-toes. And try not to wobble!

A piper in the streets today
Set up and tuned, and started to play,
And away, away, away on the tide
Of his music we started; on every side
Doors and windows were opened wide,
And men left down their work and came,
And women with petticoats coloured like flame
And little bare feet that were blue with cold,
Went dancing back to the age of gold,
And all the world went gay, went gay,
For half an hour in the street today.

What's the smallest animal you can think of? And what's the largest? The elephant perhaps?

The Kind Elephant

PAT GIBSON

One fine morning an elephant was taking a quiet walk through a wood. All at once a little mouse came running towards him looking very frightened.

"Hello," said the elephant, "you do look worried. Is there anything wrong?"

"Yes," replied the mouse, "cat is after me and I've nowhere to hide."

"Oh dear," said the elephant, who was very kind. "You may hide in my ear if you wish."

"Oh thank you," said the mouse, and he ran up the elephant's trunk and hid in his big floppy ear.

Just at that moment the cat came running by. "Have you seen a mouse pass this way?" he asked the elephant.

"A mouse," said the elephant, "what kind of a mouse?"

The cat was silent because he didn't know what kind of a mouse he was chasing. He'd smelt a mouse, but all that he'd seen was the twitch of a whisker and the flick of a tail. Then the elephant started to hum a tune.

The cat looked round him. "I wish I knew where that mouse was," he said. The elephant just went on humming – then suddenly he stopped humming and burst into laughter! Why do you think he did that? It was because the mouse was moving and his whiskers were tickling the elephant's ear! The elephant shook with laughter. The cat looked most surprised. He had no idea why the elephant was laughing, but seeing him laugh so heartily made the cat laugh too, and soon both elephant and cat were roaring with laughter. Every time the little mouse moved in the elephant's ear, his whiskers tickled even more and set off another great boom of laughter from the elephant.

By now the cat was rolling on the ground laughing. Suddenly he stopped, and wiped the tears from his whiskers. All at once he felt very tired. "I think I'll go home and have a nice long sleep," he said. "All that laughing has made me tired. I'm even too tired now to look for that mouse." And off he went back to his home.

As soon as the cat had turned his back, the mouse came out of the elephant's ear and ran down his trunk. "Thank you," he said, sitting on the tip of the elephant's trunk. "You are kind."

"That's all right," said the elephant. "Oh, excuse me yawning – I'm tired with laughing so much."

"Well, goodbye," said the mouse, and was about to go when he turned to the elephant and said: "By the way, why *were* you laughing so much?"

The elephant smiled: "Oh, nothing really, little mouse – goodbye." And he lay down to sleep.

* * *

Are you ticklish?

In the middle of my back there's a tickle,
And I really want to give it such a scratch.
But no matter how I twist and turn and wriggle,
I never ever reach that tickly patch!

Do you live in the town or the country? What do you think it's like for someone who lives in the country to visit the town for the first time?

Question Mark

MICHAEL SULLIVAN &
JUDY WHITFIELD

Mark lived in a quiet country village. But one day Mark's grandmother said she would take him up to town.

Mark was very excited as he had never been "up to town" before. Early the next morning they caught the country bus to the next village.

"Is this the town?" asked Mark.

"Not yet," said Gran.

"Why are we getting off here?" he asked.

"Because we can catch a train up to town from this village," said Gran.

The train carried them past fields and woods and country lanes, then gradually it changed, and there were only buildings and streets to be seen.

Mark had never seen a big town before. "Where are the fields and cows?" he asked.

"They went a long time ago," said Gran.

"Why?" asked Mark.

"People needed somewhere to live," said Gran.

"What are those very tall houses?" asked Mark.

"They are blocks of flats," said Gran. "Like lots of homes on top of each other."

"Are we nearly there?" asked Mark.

"Yes," said Gran. "All these questions – you really are a Question Mark today, Mark!"

The train slowed down. "Is this the station? Are we getting off? Where's the door?" Mark asked.

"Yes. Yes. The door is this way," said Gran.

They stepped off the train, and so did hundreds of other people. Everyone was hurrying in the same direction, and it was very noisy.

"Come along," said Gran, "hold my hand, then you won't get lost."

Outside the station they caught a bus. Mark had never seen one like it before. "Why has this bus got a staircase?" he asked.

"Because there's an upstairs. It's a double-decker bus. Come along, we'll go up."

"Why is there an upstairs?"

"Because, Question Mark, buses in towns have to carry lots of people."

Upstairs, Mark loved looking through the window. There were so many people, and he didn't know any of them. In the village where he lived he knew everyone.

"Who are all those people?" he asked.

"I don't know," said Gran. "You really are a Question Mark today. Come on, we're getting off the bus now."

They went down the stairs and on to the busy pavement.

"This is the shop," said Gran, and they

went through big, heavy doors, into the biggest room Mark had ever seen.

"Why are we going in here?" asked Mark.

"Because you need some new shoes and I
need a jumper," said Gran, walking over to
press a button on a wall.

"Why are you doing that?" asked Mark.

"Because then the lift will come and these
doors will open and we can go up to the fourth
floor," said Gran. Mark had never been in a
lift before. He held Gran's hand tight all the
way.

On the fourth floor they bought Mark some new shoes and then they got back into the lift. "Where are we going now?" asked Mark.

"Down to the third floor, to the Women's Department," said Gran.

Mark's Gran looked at lots and lots of jumpers. She talked to a lady in a black dress who carried some jumpers over to a place like a tent with curtains in front of it. Mark and his grandmother followed.

"Can I came into this tent with you?" asked Mark.

"I'm afraid there isn't room for both of us, Question Mark," said Gran. "You sit on the chair. I won't be long."

When Gran came out she looked different, thought Mark. "I'll take this one," she said to the lady in the black dress.

Mark popped his head through the curtains to see where Gran had been. On the wall was a very long mirror and on a chair were Gran's spectacles. That's why she looked so different, thought Mark! He picked them up carefully and took them to his grandmother.

"Why did you leave your glasses in there?" he asked.

"Thank you, Question Mark. I forgot them. I expect you'll be asking me if I've still got your new shoes."

"No I won't," said Mark. "I've got them."

"Oh good," said his grandmother. "Now where's the lift?"

"I know the answer to that one," said Mark. "Follow me."

And Gran did.

* * *

Look round the room and think of as many questions as you can about the things in it. Here's a poem about someone who's always asking questions:

I'm just going out for a moment.
Why?
To make a cup of tea.
Why?
Because I'm thirsty.
Why?
Because it's hot.
Why?
Because the sun's shining.
Why?
Because it's summer.

Why?
Because that's when it is.
Why?
Why don't you stop saying why?
Why?
Tea-time why.
High-time-you-stopped-saying-whytime.
What?

Do you live in a house or a flat? What do you think it is made of? Cat found out what his new house was made of – he was there when it was being built.

Cat's New House

MARION GREEN

Cat was there – on the building site, when the men arrived for work one morning. He sat in the dug-out foundations of the house, looking as though he belonged there. He was there the next morning and the morning after, and the morning after that.

The workmen became quite used to him, and gave him milk when they made their tea, and left-over sandwiches when they had eaten their lunch. There was lots of noise, but Cat didn't mind. He sat tight.

When the men mixed concrete and spread it, all wet and shiny, Cat put out one paw and made an imprint. The paw-mark set hard and would probably be there for ever.

When the bricklayers began to lay bricks to make the walls, he climbed higher with each new row. He sat on the top and looked at

everyone else working. Sometimes he jumped through the gaps where the windows would be.

When the joiners came with timber for the floorboards, the window frames and the roof, he climbed higher still, and scrambled in and out while they hammered each piece into place.

When the slaters came to cover in the roof, he climbed even higher, and slithered down the slates as they were laid in position one on top of another.

When the glaziers began to put glass into the window frames, he came down from the roof and sat on a window sill, looking out. He saw the plumbers who came with baths and wash basins and taps. He saw the heating engineers who came with pipes and radiators.

46

He saw the men from the Gas Board, the Electricity Board and the Water Board.

All these people came, and then went away again. But Cat didn't go away. He sat tight.

He saw the men who came with rolls of wallpaper and tins of paint and paste. Cat put out one paw and made an imprint in the paste. The paw-mark set hard and would probably be there for ever.

He saw the men who came with carpets and rugs and spread them on the new floors. And he saw the men who came in a large furniture van and carried chairs and tables and beds into the new rooms.

It was very quiet when they'd all gone away again, but Cat didn't mind. He sat tight on the new rug, on the new carpet, in the new room of his new house, and waited.

Presently, there was the noise of a car pulling up outside. Cat could hear the car door being slammed, the gate opening, footsteps along the path, and the key being turned in the lock. He could hear children's voices as they came rushing along the new hall, through the new kitchen and the new dining-room, and into the new sitting-room where he was sitting tight on the new rug.

"There's a cat!" shrieked the small girl loudly. "Here in *our* new house."

Cat twitched his whiskers disdainfully. It was *his* new house. He'd supervised the building right from the foundations to the furnishing. His paw-marks were set in the house and would probably be there for ever! Then the girl put out her hand and began to stroke

him. Cat began to purr happily.

Now at last his new house, with its new walls and roof and windows, its new carpets and chairs and curtains and his new paw-marks which would probably be there for ever – was no longer just his new *house*. It was his new *home*.

*　　*　　*

Try building a wall out of old boxes . . . see how many you can balance on top of each other before they fall down. Cats often like to sit on high walls, because they can see what's going on. But not every cat wants a home – some are alley-cats.

A bit of jungle in the street
He goes on velvet toes,
And slinking through the shadows, stalks
Imaginary foes.

Do you have a favourite jumper or T-shirt? King Timothy liked the jumpers the Queen knitted.

Knit One, Purl One

SUSAN EAMES

The Queen was watching television in the palace lounge when the door opened and in walked King Timothy, wearing very muddy wellingtons.

"Stop," she cried, "just look at your boots!"

The King looked. "Oh dear," he said. "I'm sorry, I forgot."

"Forgot! That's the third time this week you've come in with dirty boots. There's mud all over the carpet." She rang for a servant to clear up the mess. "Just you go out again and take them off," she said crossly.

Poor King Timothy! He turned and trudged out, leaving clods of mud behind him. The Queen was right. He *did* keep coming in with his boots on, but he didn't mean to be a nuisance. It was just that he forgot to take the boots off at the back door. A few minutes later when he returned to the lounge to look for his slippers the Queen said: "If you come in wearing muddy boots once more I'll ... I'll ... I'll stop knitting pullovers for you."

Now the King's pullovers were so lovely they were known throughout the land. The Queen knitted each one herself, so there were no others like them anywhere. The King was very proud of them, and for several days he remembered to change before going into the palace. Then, one day, he did some gardening, and dashed inside to show the Queen a very hairy caterpillar that he'd found on one of his cabbages. But – his boots. He had forgotten to take them off!

"No more pullovers," said the Queen.

"But, but, but ..." spluttered King Timothy.

"No more."

King Timothy climbed the stairs to his private room at the top of the palace, and sat down to think. He would miss having no more pullovers to show off. So he said to himself: "If the Queen's not making any more then I shall have to knit them myself." He had seen her knitting and there didn't seem to be much to it. All he needed was some needles, wool and a pattern.

"I'll show her I can knit my own pullovers. Anyone can knit!" he muttered. And he rang the bell for his servant.

Later, the servant came back with some thick knitting needles, several balls of wool and a pattern, and handed them to the King.

King Timothy stayed in his private room all the afternoon and late into the night. The servant waited outside. All he could hear was the sound of needles clicking and sometimes: "Tch. Bother!" when the King dropped a stitch.

Next day the King had breakfast in his room. By lunchtime he had knitted himself a pullover. The Queen had hardly finished banging the gong to summon him to lunch when he came down the stairs wearing his new pullover.

But the right sleeve was much too long. It was almost a foot longer than the left one. Although the King kept pushing it up it would slip down, and each time somebody was introduced to him and went to shake hands they could not find his hand. They only shook a handful of sleeve. King Timothy thought it was a huge joke, but the Queen did not laugh. Then the neck was much too big,

and although he kept pushing it down it would jump up again. Sometimes King Timothy found it difficult to see where he was going and fell over the furniture.

So the Queen (who was a very kind person really and didn't want him to hurt himself) decided to forgive him. She knitted the King a new pullover and then he almost never went into the palace wearing dirty muddy boots again.

But when he did, the Queen looked the other way.

*   *   *

Don't forget to wear wellington boots to go out in the mud – and don't forget to take them off when you come back inside!

In the dark it's very difficult to walk in a straight line.

Mr Josh Jolly goes Camping

JOYCE TOMSETT

In a country called Calimba lived a very important man. His name was Mr Josh Jolly and it was his job to look out from the top-most turret of the castle and tell the King of Calimba when anyone was coming.

It was time for a summer holiday at the castle and the King was going to visit some neighbours. "If you are wise, you will do the same," he said to Mr Josh Jolly.

"Oh dear," said Mr Josh Jolly, "I'd love to go on a summer holiday, but where shall I go?" Living all alone in the top-most turret of Calimba Castle, he had no one near whom he could really call a friend.

"The royal children are going camping, why don't you join them?" suggested the King.

"What a splendid idea," said Mr Josh Jolly, and he began to collect the things a camper needs.

He took:
a penknife,
a box of matches,
a map,
a compass,
a change of clothing,
and *two* extra pairs of socks.
A first-aid box,
a cup and a plate,
a knife, fork and spoon,
a sleeping bag,
and a big brown waterproof cape.

He packed everything into a haversack except the sleeping bag and the cape, these he rolled up and strapped on top. Then he hoisted the haversack on his back and joined the royal children in the courtyard.

"Goodbye," said the King.

"Keep your feet dry," said the Queen.

"Don't get lost," shouted the royal servants and soldiers.

"Get lost!" said Mr Josh Jolly. "Get lost! I am a very good camper. Of course we won't get lost."

And they all waved goodbye.

Off they went, over the drawbridge, down the lane and into the forest. The forest was rather dark and gloomy and Mr Josh Jolly

looked over his shoulder nervously, but the royal children were not a bit worried.

"We shall never get lost, heigh-ho, hooray for Mr Josh Jolly," they sang.

As the trees became bigger and the path became narrower, Mr Josh Jolly began to wish that he had stayed in the top-most turret. He was getting very tired.

"I think we will camp here," he said, stopping under a big tree.

"Oh no!" said the children. "There is no room here for a tent," and they were quite right.

So they went on, for miles and miles, or so it seemed to Mr Josh Jolly. At last they came to an opening in the trees. But by the time they pitched the tent it was quite dark, and even the lively royal children were glad to crawl inside the tent and sleep.

Next morning Mr Josh Jolly awoke with a start. What was that noise? Sleepily he made his way from the tent and rubbed his eyes. He soon realised that the noise was laughter, lots of laughter. The royal children were laughing, and the servants and soldiers were laughing. Everyone was laughing because Mr Josh Jolly and the children had walked so far that they had walked round in a circle and got back to the castle again. He'd pitched the tent beside the castle near the drawbridge, and right underneath his own top-most turret.

"Well, I see you didn't get lost," said the King.

"No, we didn't get lost," said Mr Josh Jolly, laughing the loudest of all.

* * *

Follow my Bangalorey Man
Follow my Bangalorey Man!
I'll do all that ever I can
To follow my Bangalorey Man.
We'll borrow a horse and steal a gig,
And round the world we'll do a jig,
And I'll do all that ever I can
To follow my Bangalorey Man.

Do you forget things, and tie a knot in your handkerchief to help you remember . . . don't forget the forgetful king!

The King's Handkerchief

Once there was a King who was very forgetful. Sometimes he couldn't even remember where he'd put his crown and would look everywhere for it. On his desk . . . in his cupboard . . . on the dining-table. It wasn't to be found. Then when he bent down to look under his throne it would fall off his head where it had been all the time!

Then he had an idea. As he was so forgetful, when he wanted to remind himself of something particularly important he would tie a knot in his handkerchief.

Well, one day, the King was sitting in his throne room, thinking of nothing in particular, when he felt a sneeze coming on. Quickly he pulled out his handkerchief and sneezed. But as he was just about to put it back in his pocket he saw that there were no less than *four* knots in his handkerchief—one at each corner.

"Goodness me," he exclaimed. "There must have been something very important to remember to make me tie *four* knots in a handkerchief. I wonder what it was?"

The King thought about it all day, but he couldn't remember. When evening came and he was sitting down to dinner with the Princess he asked her: "Tell me, my dear, have you any idea why I have four knots in my handkerchief?"

"Four knots! No, I can't think of anything," said the Princess.

All that night the King sat and tried to remember. By the morning he was very tired and very cross. He decided he would write out an announcement: *Whoever can tell me why I made the four knots shall marry the Princess.* He put the notice on the throne and the handkerchief in front of it and sat down in another chair to wait.

The news went round the palace like wildfire; everybody wanted to marry the Princess, so they all tried very hard to guess why the King had tied the four knots. The first person to call on him was the Prime Minister.

The Prime Minister was wearing a dark suit and a bowler hat and carrying a rolled umbrella. He picked up the handkerchief and said: "Your Majesty, you tied four knots in your handkerchief to remind you to come to a meeting with the Government."

"Nonsense!" said the King. "I hate meetings – I shouldn't *want* to remember to go to one."

So the Prime Minister couldn't marry the Princess. Next to try was the King's secretary who wrote all the King's letters for him. He came in with a quill pen behind his ear and roll of parchment in his hand.

The secretary bowed very low and picked up the handkerchief and said: "Your Majesty, I think you tied four knots to remind you to write a letter to your brother."

"Nonsense!" said the King. "I hate writing letters – I shouldn't want to remember to write to my brother."

So the secretary couldn't marry the Princess. Next to try was the Palace Chef. He came in wearing his long white apron and his tall chef's hat and carrying a jelly on a plate.

The chef bowed very low and picked up the handkerchief and said: "Your Majesty, I think you tied four knots to remind you to ask for your favourite jelly for tea – and I've brought it – orange jelly."

"Nonsense!" said the King. "I'm fed up with jellies – particularly orange jellies – I shouldn't want to remember that."

By the end of that day, everybody in the Palace had tried to guess why the King had tied four knots in his handkerchief. Well – almost everybody!

One person who had been working too hard to read the King's announcement, was the youngest of the King's gardeners. So the King sent for him.

He came in wearing a long brown overall and muddy boots. He bowed low and said: "Good evening, your Majesty! How can I help you?"

"I want to know why I tied four knots in this handkerchief," said the King. "I'm tired of people making up ridiculous explanations, and if you guess wrongly I shall have you dismissed."

"I don't have to guess your Majesty," answered the gardener. "You were walking in the garden yesterday . . ."

"Yes, yes I was!"

"And the sun was rather hot, so you took out your handkerchief and tied knots in the corner to cover your head from the sun. Like this." And the gardener put the handkerchief on his head.

"You're right! I know you're right!" said the King. "And you shall be the one to marry the Princess."

Then the gardener gave the King his handkerchief, and the King untied the knots and put it into his pocket.

Next day, there was a great procession of sparkling coaches and spanking horses when the Princess, followed by all her attendants, rode out from the Palace to her wedding with the gardener. And they both lived happily ever after.

The King was still forgetful – but he could always ask his son-in-law for help.

*   *   *

King's cross
What shall we do?
His purple robe
Is rent in two!
Out of his Crown
He's torn the gems!
He's thrown the Sceptre
Into the Thames!

Have you ever seen a horse and cart?
There are still some about on the
roads, although nearly all deliveries
are made by vans and lorries. But one
day horses might come back . . .

The Milkman and his Horse

JENNY O'MAHONY

Everyone knew Fred the milkman. All the
other milkmen had smart, electric milk floats,
but Fred still had an old cart which was
pulled by an old horse. And the horse's name
was Dobbin.

When Fred went whistling along the roads,
delivering milk bottles, all the children came
out of their houses to see Dobbin. Sometimes
they brought him a carrot, sometimes a piece
of bread. Sometimes they couldn't bring him
anything to eat at all, so they just came and
talked to him.

The other milkmen laughed at Fred.
"Look at your old cart," they said, "and your
old horse! Why don't you get a new electric
milk float?"

But Fred didn't want one. "I can't talk to

an electric milk float," he said to Dobbin, "but I can talk to you."

Then one day the owner of the dairy said to him: "You know, Fred, your cart's getting old, and so is Dobbin. What you need is an electric milk float like all the other milkmen. And Dobbin can go away to the country."

Fred was very sad. The owner of the dairy was getting the new milk float in five days' time. And those five days seemed to go by very quickly. On Dobbin's last day, all the children came out to say goodbye. They were sad too.

When they had delivered all the milk, Fred and Dobbin started back towards the dairy as slowly as they could because it was their last day together.

They were almost back at the dairy, when they saw one of the milkmen running up the road towards them. "I was looking for you, Fred," he panted. "My milk float won't start again and I can't deliver the milk. Please would you help me?"

"Of course!" said Fred happily. He loaded all the full milk bottles into Dobbin's cart, and put all his empty bottles into the milk float. Dobbin pulled the old cart along the roads, and Fred gave everyone their milk.

They were on their way back to the dairy
for the second time, when – would you be-
lieve it – they came across another electric
milk float that had broken down. "I've done
most of my round," said the milkman, "but
there are still a few roads to go. Please could
you deliver the rest of the milk, Fred?"

So Fred loaded more full milk bottles into
Dobbin's cart and put the empty bottles into
the broken-down electric milk float. They
were both very tired by the time they turned
round to go back to the dairy.

It was so late that Fred thought all the
other milkmen would have gone home. But as
he led Dobbin into the yard, he heard cheers
and clapping. All the other milkmen were
there, waiting to meet them.

68

"Well done, Fred! Well done, Dobbin!" said the owner of the dairy. "I don't think we can send Dobbin away after all the help he's been today."

And he took Fred and Dobbin round to the field at the back of the dairy.

"Dobbin can stay here," he said, "and so can the old cart. And if ever there's anything wrong with our milk floats, Dobbin can take over."

And that's what he did. Every so often, a milk float would break down, and Fred and Dobbin would do the round. Sometimes Fred would take Dobbin out on a Saturday or a Sunday for a treat. Then all the children would come running out for a ride in the empty cart. And they never forgot a piece of bread or a carrot or a little something for Dobbin.

The Pedlar and His Caps

(Traditional)

Once upon a time there was a pedlar, who had some hats to sell. And as he travelled from place to place he carried his hats in the easiest way he knew, all piled up on top of his one old hat which was on top of his head. One very hot day he'd been walking for miles in the sun and hadn't sold any hats, so he decided to stop and rest in the shade of a tall tree. He sat down, put all the hats except his own old one on the ground next to him, and went to sleep.

He slept for a long time, and when he woke up the first thing he did was to reach for his hats.

But they weren't there!

He still had his own old hat – but all his new hats had disappeared. He had nothing to sell to make any money.

He looked around him. There was nowhere the hats could have rolled or fallen. And they couldn't have blown away – it was a hot, windless day. Then he looked up. And there

at the top of the tree were some monkeys. And they were wearing his hats!

"Hey!" he shouted. "You monkeys, give me back my hats!" And he shook his fist at them.

But all the monkeys did was shake their paws back at him.

"Don't you shake your paws at me," he shouted. "Give me back my hats!" And he shook his other fist at the monkeys.

But all the monkeys did was shake their other paws back at him.

"Don't you shake your other paws at me!" shouted the pedlar. "Give me back my hats." And he shook both his fists at the monkeys.

But all the monkeys did was shake both their paws back at him. They were making fun of the pedlar by copying everything that he did. That gave him an idea.

He looked at the monkeys, and shouted: "This is your last chance, monkeys. Give me back my hats!"

Then he took off his own hat and threw it on the ground. And all the monkeys copied him.

The pedlar picked up the hats, and set off to sell them at the next village.

"Thank you monkeys!" he shouted. "Goodbye!" And he waved to them. And the monkeys waved back.

*   *   *

I tried on a hat with a feather upon it,
And everyone said –
What a beautiful bonnet!

I tried on a hat with a blue and green whatnot,
And everyone said –
What a beautiful topknot!

I tried on a hat that everyone hated,
They said that I really looked quite
Addle-pated!

But I liked it best, for it had a big veil –
So I bought it and left the two others for sale!

The Jungle Sale

LEE PRESSMAN

One Saturday morning, Sally and her mother were out shopping. On the way back Sally's mother stopped to chat to her friend Mrs Lee. As they were saying goodbye she said: "Don't forget the jumble sale today. It starts at two o'clock at the church hall."

"I'll see you there," said Mrs Lee. "We might get some good bargains."

What's that, thought Sally as they went home. A JUNGLE SALE! Did she say a Jungle Sale? That's good. Perhaps I'll be able to buy a baby elephant or chimpanzee! I must tell Thomas.

So she rushed off to find her friend, and she discovered him lying on the pavement, watching an ant that was struggling to drag a huge leaf behind it.

"Hello Sally," he said.

"Hello Thomas! I've got some great news. They're holding a Jungle Sale at the church hall at two o'clock. You must come."

"What's a Jungle Sale?" asked Thomas.

"Well, I'm not sure,' said Sally, "but I

73

suppose it must be where they sell all jungle things like animals and trees."

"But I've only got two pence," replied Thomas.

"Doesn't matter," said Sally. "You'll probably be able to buy a baby parrot or something small. Now go and tell everyone else." So Thomas went off and told Amelia. She didn't know what a Jungle Sale was either, so he explained and she promised to come. Then she told Edward and Earl, and *they* told Alice and *she* told Penny. By two o'clock, there was a whole crowd of children waiting outside the church hall, all grasping money in their hands.

"What are you all doing here?" asked Sally's mother, who was in a queue of grown-ups.

"We're waiting to buy some animals and things at the Jungle Sale," answered Sally proudly.

All the grown-ups burst out laughing. "It's not a *Jungle* Sale, it's a *Jumble* Sale!" said Sally's mother.

"What's that?" asked Thomas.

"Jumble means all sorts of bits and pieces that no one wants any more. They're all collected up and sold cheaply," replied Sally's mother.

"No lions?" enquired Edward.

"No alligators?" asked Penny.

"Not even a baby parrot for two pence?" said Thomas.

"I'm afraid not," said Mrs Lee. "But come in anyway. I'm sure you'll find something you like."

And they did.

Sally bought an old train with one wheel missing.

Thomas bought a book.

Amelia bought a necklace.

Edward and Earl put their money together and bought a football.

Penny bought a walking stick.

Alice bought a picture of the queen.

They all thought it had been a very good jumble sale – even without the animals.

*　　*　　*

Jungle sounds like jumble! Can you think of words that sound like the toys' names – like Bed and Ted or Bramble and Hamble?

Different birds build different kinds of nest. Have you seen where birds nest – in bushes, trees, on lamp-posts, even under the guttering on houses?

The Magpie's Nest

MICHAEL ROSEN

Once a long time ago, when winter was nearly over and spring had nearly begun, all the birds were busy starting to build their nests. There they all were: the robin and the eagle, the seagull, the blackbird, the duck, the owl and the humming bird, all busy. All, that is, except Magpie. And she didn't feel much like working.

It was a nice day and she was out and about looking for scrips and scraps and bibs and bobs for her collection of old junk – her hoard of bits and pieces she had picked up from behind chimneys or from drain-pipes. Pebbles, beads, buttons and the like, any-thing bright and interesting or unusual, Mag-pie was sure to collect. Just as she was flying along on the look-out for a new treasure, she caught sight of Sparrow, her mouth full of bits

of straw and twigs.

"What are you doing, what are you doing?" said Magpie.

"Building my nest," said Sparrow, "like you'll have to soon."

"Oh yes?" said Magpie.

"Yes," said Sparrow, "put that milk-bottle-top down and come over here and watch. First you have to find a twig, and then another-twig, another-twig, another-twig, another-twig . . ."

"Don't make me laugh," said Magpie, "I know, I know, I know all that," and off she flew. And as she flew on looking for scrips and scraps and bibs and bobs she came up to Duck who was upside down with her mouth full of mud.

78

"What are you doing, what are you doing?" said Magpie.

"Building my nest," said Duck, "like you'll have to soon."

"Oh yes?" said Magpie.

"Yes," said Duck, "throw away that old earwig and watch me. After you've got all your twigs you have to stick them with mud pats like this – pat-pat, pat-pat, pat-pat . . ."

"Don't make me laugh," said Magpie, "I know, I know, I know all that," and off she flew. And as she flew on looking for scrips and scraps and bibs and bobs she saw Pigeon with a mouthful of feathers.

"What are you doing, what are you doing?" said Magpie.

"Building my nest," said Pigeon, "like you'll have to soon."

"Oh yes?" said Magpie.

"Yes," said Pigeon, "put that bus ticket down and come over here and learn how. You have to make yourself warm and cosy – right? Right. So you dig your beak into your chest like this – right? And find one of those very soft, fluffy, feathers down there and you lay that out very carefully inside your nest to keep it warm-and-cosy, warm-and-cosy, warm-and-cosy . . ."

"Don't make me laugh," said Magpie, "I know, I know, I know, I know all that," and off she flew.

Well, not long after that it was time for Magpie to lay her eggs and she looked out from her perch and saw all the other birds sitting in their well-built, warm, cosy nests, laying their eggs. "Oh no," said Magpie, "I haven't got anywhere to lay mine! I'd better hurry." And she remembered Sparrow saying something about twigs, and Duck about patting them and Pigeon saying something about cosy feathers. So she rushed out and quickly grabbed as many twigs as she could, made a great pile of them, threw a feather on the top – and the milk-bottle-top and the earwig and the bus ticket and she *just* had time to sit herself down and lay her eggs.

And if you look at a magpie's nest you'll see it's always a mess. And she ends up throwing her scrips and scraps and bibs and bobs in it too.

I think she likes it like that.

*   *   *

Magpies are usually seen in twos or threes. Perhaps that is why it's supposed to be unlucky to see one on its own. There's an old rhyme about magpies:

One for sorrow,
Two for joy,
Three for a girl,
Four for a boy.

In this country it's good to live in a solid house which will keep out the cold and damp, but in other parts of the world it's not always the same.

The Camel's House

JOANNE COLE

There was once a man called Bedu living with his family on the edge of the desert. There were two boys who used to look after the sheep, and take them to look for grass.

All around them was the dry and dusty desert, and here and there the tents of other families. Bedu's tent looked as if it was made from rags, but it was strong, and kept out the wind, the sun, and the rain – when it rained, which wasn't often. Bedu liked living in the tent, he had lived in a tent all his life.

Bedu's family had two donkeys who always stayed near the tent, and a dog, as well as the sheep.

And, most important of all, Bedu had a camel. He was very proud of his camel, and whenever he had to go on a long journey, he would ride on it.

One day a rich man came from a distant city to visit Bedu. He was a kind person who liked to help others. When he saw how Bedu lived he said to himself: "I have a floor, windows, walls, ceiling, a roof, a chimney, taps, basins, baths . . . all these things I have, but Bedu just has a tent."

When he got back to the city he bought Bedu a house – one of those houses that comes in pieces to be put together – and had it sent out to him on a lorry. And when it was put together Bedu too had a floor, walls, ceiling, windows and roof. He took his family to live in the new house.

But he didn't like it.

He missed seeing the sky through the top of his tent.

He missed seeing the sides of his tent move in the wind.

So he decided to give the house to his camel to live in. "It will keep him warm in the winter," he said.

And Bedu and his family went back to live in their tent, and the camel slept in the house.

And they are still living there now, looking after their animals in the desert.

*　　*　　*

You could pretend to be a camel, on hands and feet – not knees – and move along slowly – waving your jaws from side to side.

I'm a humpity camel and I walk very slow,
I'm a bumpity camel and I don't want to go
Anywhere till you give me my tea!
Just give me buns and cakes,
And lots of chocolate flakes,
And then I promise you'll see,
What a nice camel I'll be!

Have you noticed that on some days *everything* seems to make a noise? Nothing happens without a bang or a bump – even waking up.

Bumpy Day

NICK WILSON

Clang, bang, bump, bump,
Bottles on the step.
Time to get up!
Oh bother!
Bump – ow! Toe on the bed!
Quick! Clothes on!

Bump, bump, bump, bump,
Bottom down the stairs.
Bump, bump, bump, bump,
Four sit on chairs.
Morning Mum, morning Dad.

Bump, bump, bump, bump,
Eggs for breakfast
Bang, bang, bang, on the door,
Bump, bump, bump, on the floor
Three letters – thump – oops one more!

Bump, there's the paper
Bump, through the door!
Bump, bump, down the stairs
Bump, bump, bump, two more.

Off with a roar.
Through the traffic
Bump, bump, stop!
Bump, open the door.
Bye Dad!
Bump, on the back!
Hello, Alvin!

Bump, bump, two sit building
Tower of bricks – watch out!
Bump, bumpity, bump, bump, bump,
All fall down!
What next?
Parp, parp, bump! Mind where you go.
Two box cars, wheel to toe!
Never mind!
Crunch, crunch,
An apple for lunch!

Bang, bang, bump, bump,
Climb on the see-saw
What an uproar!
See-saw Marjorie daw,
Bump,
Johnny shall have a new master,
Bump,
He shall have but a penny a day,
Bump,
Because he can't work any faster.

Bump,
End of the day
No more play.

Where's Mum?
Oh, there she is!
Bump, bump, in the pushchair.
Bump, down the road!
Bump, down the kerb!
Stop – bump on the button!
Wait for green.

Quick, cross the road!
Bump, bump, nearly home!
Bump, through the gate.
Bump, through the door,
Bump, bump, on the stairs.
Time for tea.

Bump, bump, bump,
Up the stairs on a back
Face washed,
Teeth cleaned.
Bump, bump, shoes by the bed.
Pyjamas on, what a tired head!
Bump, bump, bump, Mum down the stairs.
What a bumpy day!
Sleepy eyes shut tight
Nothing goes bump in the night.

*   *   *

Mrs Slam-bang stamped *down the stairs*
And slammed *on her hat*
And stamped *into her boots*
And heaved *open the door*
And slam-banged *the door shut*
And slam-banged, slam-banged *all*
The way down the street to catch her bus.

Sometimes it gets very crowded and hot and uncomfortable on buses.

One Hot Day

GRACE READ

Barney was driving his big red bus, taking people to work as usual.

"Hurry along!" cried the conductor when they stopped to pick up some more passengers.

Old Mrs Marsh puffed, hauling herself up the step: "Can't hurry . . . it's much too 'ot!" she said.

It really was a scorcher. The conductor mopped his brow. Usually he joked with his customers, but this morning he didn't feel like it.

He growled at little Andrew Brown, who had been crying. "And what's that funny face for?"

"Oh, he wanted to go to the paddling pool instead of coming to the sales with me," Andrew's mother explained.

After her came a young lady teacher who was annoyed because she had torn her tights.

Then there was a nice young man who was sad because no one had remembered his birthday.

Lastly there was a grumpy bank manager who'd had to run for the bus because his car had broken down.

What long faces Barney thought, watching them. If I get all of them to work quickly . . . perhaps that will cheer them up!

But there was so much traffic that the journey took even longer than usual, and the passengers grew hotter and crosser. Old Mrs Marsh came over quite faint and had to be fanned with a newspaper.

Presently the bus came to a complete standstill where workmen were mending the road. A policeman was sending all the traffic a longer way round.

Most of the passengers started scowling and fidgeting and groaning. But old Mrs Marsh said she didn't care *which* way the bus went, so long as they could find some FRESH AIR.

Some fresh air? That was what everyone needed, thought Barney. He was feeling extremely hot himself. So instead of following all the other traffic crawling towards the city, he nipped smartly down a side street. Pretty soon they were out of the crush and rolling along the highway.

"Hey! This don't look right!" The conductor pinged his bell sharply. But Barney just kept right on going.

Through the windows the passengers were amazed to see things like cows in fields, and buttercups and daisies. There was a gentle breeze blowing. It made them all feel so happy they didn't care that the bus was travelling the *wrong way*.

Soon everyone was smiling and chatting to everyone else. And when the bus turned a corner and they saw *the sea* – with the sun sparkling on it, everybody cheered.

Barney drove them right down to a sandy bay before he stopped.

"All change for a paddle," the conductor

called merrily.

Out tumbled the travellers, whipping off shoes and stockings and rolling up trouser legs.

"Ooh! It's a bit chilly," giggled old Mrs Marsh, dipping her toes in.

The young lady teacher and the nice young man held hands as they paddled.

The conductor made paper boats for Andrew to sail and his mother found lots of pretty shells.

The bank manager knotted a handkerchief over his head and treated everyone to ice-cream.

Barney had a lovely snooze and woke up feeling great. He sounded his horn to say . . . wasn't it about time they got back to work?

Everyone crowded around him to say thank you for the unexpected treat. It had done them good.

The nice young man said it was the best birthday he'd ever had.

The young lady teacher was thrilled when Andrew's mother gave her some shells to show to her class at school.

And when old Mrs Marsh started singing in the bus they all joined in and sang all the way back to town.

The traffic jams had only just been sorted out by the time they arrived, so they were no later than other people getting to work.

The bank manager beamed at his staff. They couldn't understand why he was in such a good mood on this hot day. But then, of course, they didn't know about the sand in his trouser turn-ups.

* * *

What sort of thing cheers up you?

Girls and boys come out to play,
The moon doth shine as bright as day,
Leave your supper and leave your sleep,
And come with your playfellows into the street.
Come with a whoop, come with a call,
Come with a goodwill or not at all.
Up the ladder and down the wall,
A half-penny roll will serve us all.
You find milk, and I'll find flour,
And we'll have a pudding in half-an-hour.

Has anybody ever winked at you? Usually it's the sign of a joke – or maybe just because somebody likes you! The boy in the story wanted to wink.

I Wish I Could Wink

JUDY WHITFIELD

Once there was a boy called Tom Fisher. Some of his friends could wink – and so could lots of grown-ups he knew.

One was the man in the paper shop. "Morning Mrs Fisher," he would say, "morning Tom. No comics this week I'm afraid." And he would give Tom a big wink. Tom knew that the comics had arrived, really, and the paper man was joking.

The lady in the baker's always had a wink for him too. "Hello," she would say, "ten loaves of bread is it today?" and she would give him just a little wink, which meant she really knew that Tom's mother bought only one loaf.

The lollipop man on the zebra crossing always gave Tom a wink. He would stop all the cars and wave as Tom and his mother

crossed – and just as Tom went past, the
lollipop man would peer at him from under
his hat and look surprised and say: "You're a
big lad – shouldn't you be at school?" and
wink, which meant that he really knew Tom
wasn't quite old enough to be at school yet.

When Tom's mother had done all the
shopping in the supermarket, the lady at the
checkout who wore big earrings would say to

Tom: "Are you carrying all this home for your Mum?" Then she'd wink, and Tom knew that she knew the shopping was all going into the basket on his pushchair.

"I wish I could wink," thought Tom as he sat in his pushchair. He tried to wink all the way home. But somehow, however hard he tried, when he closed one eye, the other one closed as well. Then he tried to do it very gently, but again, both of his eyes closed. From that time, whenever Tom went into the paper shop: *No comics this week*, or saw the lady in the baker's shop: *Ten loaves today?*, or met the lollipop man: *Shouldn't you be at school?*, or smiled at the lady in the supermarket: *Are you carrying all that home?*, he watched them all very carefully, and realised they each had their own special way of winking.

So Tom decided he'd have *his* own special way of winking. It didn't always work – sometimes both of his eyes closed – but nobody seemed to notice.

And one day, when it was pouring with rain, Tom said to the lollipop man: "Isn't it a lovely day?" and winked a real wink.

And the lollipop man winked back!

*   *   *

If you can't wink, you can always
pull a funny face.

Pull a funny face,
Move your eyes and nose and mouth
All over the place.
First you smile like a clown.
Then you turn the corners down.
Bare your teeth, open wide,
Move your jaws from side to side.

Pull a funny face,
Move your eyes and nose and mouth
All over the place.
Raise your eyebrows, roll your eyes,
Make them grow to twice their size,
Shut them tight, wink and blink,
Keep them open just a chink.

Pull a funny face,
Move your eyes and nose and mouth,
All over the place.

In the animal world winter can be
hard and cruel. But sometimes creatures can help one another survive.

The Sheep and the Bird

WENDY EYTON

It was winter-time and the snow was falling
thick and fast on the hill slopes. There were
no trees on the hill slopes, and the sheep
huddled for shelter behind a stone wall. The
snow was so deep it covered the bodies of the
sheep, and only their heads peeped out.

Sheep have warm woolly coats, and most of
them did not mind the snow too much. But
one old sheep did mind it. Years of being out
in all weathers had made him stiff in the
joints – that is, once he sat down he found it
hard to get up again. And this sheep looked
up at the cold grey sky, at the thickly falling
snow, shivered, and felt very miserable.

Then, through the snowy silence, he heard
a sound and one snowflake, bigger than the
others, seemed to be coming nearer and nearer. The old sheep shook the snow from his
eyelids and opened his eyes wide. It was not a

snowflake at all, but a small bird. And the bird was singing to him.

"Cheer up! Cheer up! The warm west wind is coming. I can hear it in the distance. The warm west wind will melt away the snow."

And the small bird sang such a beautiful song that the old sheep forgot his cold nose and his stiffened joints. When the bird stopped singing and flew away he remembered them again, but he thought to himself: "The warm west wind is coming. The bird said so."

And in a day or two a wind did come from across warm seas. It blew away the snow from the air, and on the ground the snow began to melt into water and trickle away.

The old sheep stood up slowly, two legs at a time, shook himself, and began to nose for tufts of grass beneath the melting snow. But still he shivered, for his coat was wet and the air was very cold.

Then he pricked up his ears. The small bird was flying close to him. "Cheer up! Cheer up! The spring is coming. I can hear it in the distance. The spring will come and make the flowers bloom!"

The small bird sang her beautiful song again, and the old sheep quite forgot his wet coat and stiffened joints. "Spring is coming," he said, as he nibbled the grass beneath the snow. "The bird said so."

And as the last of the melted snow trickled away, tiny snowdrops began to thrust out of the earth. The sun grew warmer and dried out the old sheep's coat. The little bird flew to and fro, very busily. She was building a nest in an old thorn bush. She criss-crossed twigs, added straw from the farm and lined the nest with soft mud, which dried out in the sun.

"Now my nest is ready," she chirruped to the old sheep, "and I will lay my eggs in it."

The old sheep thought how kind the small bird had been in the cold winter days, and how she had sung her beautiful song to him.

"The weather is warmer now," he said, "and I can easily spare a little wool from my coat. Fly on to my back, take some in your beak, and line your nest with it."

The small bird knew that with a lining of sheep's wool her nest would be the cosiest place in the world for her eggs. She flew on to the sheep's back and took some strands of wool in her beak, very gently. Then she flew off to her nest with them.

The sun grew warmer and warmer, and flowers of many colours blossomed on the hill slopes. The old sheep munched on clover, his favourite treat, and the air was filled with the humming of bees.

Then one morning he heard a glorious song from the old thorn bush. The bird was singing her song again, and three tiny voices were cheeping and calling with her.

"My eggs have hatched!" sang the bird. "Spring is here! Spring is here!"

And the old sheep was very content.

*　　*　　*

Baa baa, black sheep,
Have you any wool?
Yes sir, yes sir,
Three bags full.

One for my master,
And one for my dame,
And one for the little boy
That lives down the lane.

This story in verse shows the rhythm and repetition for which this author is well-known.

The Cake

WILMA HORSBRUGH

I am the farmer, I live at Strathblane,
I plough my fields and sow my grain.

I am the miller at Campsie Glen,
I ground the corn that was cut by the men
Employed by the farmer who lives at Strathblane
Who ploughed his fields and sowed his grain.

Here is the woman who kneaded the dough,
Made from the flour as white as snow,
Bought from the miller at Campsie Glen,
Who ground the corn that was cut by the men
Employed by the farmer who lives at Strathblane
Who ploughed his fields and sowed his grain.

Here is the milk and butter as well
That came from a cow whose name is Nell,
Owned by the woman who kneaded the dough,
Made from the flour as white as snow,
Bought from the miller at Campsie Glen,
Who ground the corn that was cut by the men
Employed by the farmer who lives at Strathblane
Who ploughed his fields and sowed his grain.

Here is the hen with the yellow legs
Who provided the handsome new-laid eggs,
To mix with the milk and butter as well,
That came from the cow whose name is Nell,
Owned by the woman who kneaded the dough,
Made from the flour as white as snow,
Bought from the miller at Campsie Glen,
Who ground the corn that was cut by the men
Employed by the farmer who lives at Strathblane,
Who ploughed his fields and sowed his grain.

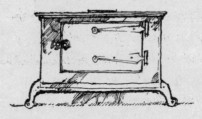

Here is the oven in which the cake
Was placed for an hour and more to bake,
Watched by the hen with the yellow legs
Who provided the handsome new-laid eggs,
To mix with the milk and butter as well
That came from the cow whose name was Nell,

Owned by the woman who kneaded the dough,
Made from the flour as white as snow,
Bought from the miller at Campsie Glen,
Who ground the corn that was cut by the men
Employed by the farmer who lives at Strathblane,
Who ploughed his fields and sowed his grain.

Here is the cake – without a doubt
Done to a turn – now lifted out
Of the nice hot oven in which the cake
Was placed for an hour and more to bake,
Watched by the hen with the yellow legs
Who provided the handsome new-laid eggs,
To mix with the milk and butter as well
That came from the cow whose name was Nell,
Owned by the woman who kneaded the dough,
Made from the flour as white as snow,
Bought from the miller at Campsie Glen,
Who ground the corn that was cut by the men
Employed by the farmer who lives at Strathblane
Who ploughed his fields and sowed his grain.

Here is the table set for tea,
With cups and plates for you and me,
And the beautiful cake – without a doubt
Done to a turn – now lifted out
Of the nice hot oven in which the cake
Was placed for an hour and more to bake,
Watched by the hen with the yellow legs
Who provided the handsome new-laid eggs,
To mix with the milk and butter as well
That came from the cow whose name is Nell,
Owned by the woman who kneaded the dough,
Made from the flour as white as snow,
Bought from the miller at Campsie Glen,
Who ground the corn that was cut by the men
Employed by the farmer of Strathblane
Who ploughed his fields and sowed his grain.

In the countryside, or in a large garden, all sorts of creatures make their homes. Mice have holes, rabbits dig burrows. But where do hedgehogs live?

Where Can I Sleep?

JEAN WATSON

"Where can I sleep? Oh, where can I sleep till the warmer weather comes?" said the hedgehog to himself one cold and windy morning.

He sat on the garden path, like a giant teasle, and looked all around the garden. Through spring and summer he had shuffled happily each evening among the lawns, hedges and flower-beds, and slept all through the day under a bush. But now that the weather was colder, all he wanted to do was to sleep all night as well as all day. The bush was too draughty and open now that its leaves had fallen – so where could he sleep and be safe and warm?

He sighed, and began to shuffle slowly here and there. Then he stopped by the tree. Perhaps he could find a hole among the roots that would be just right for a long, long sleep.

He nosed about until he had found just the right spot and then curled up with a happy and tired grunt.

But not for long.

Hoppity-skip, hoppity-skip, hoppity-skip.

What was that? The hedgehog uncurled just enough to see one, two, three, four, five little rabbits playing hide-and-seek among the roots. "There'll be no peace for me here," he thought. Slowly, he uncurled and squeezed out of the hole.

"Where can I sleep? Oh, where can I sleep?" he said, as he began to shuffle here and there again.

He stopped beside the garden shed. Something long lay on the ground. He looked down one end, and saw there was a hole right through the middle. And the hole was big enough for a hedgehog to wriggle into! Perhaps this was just the right place for a long, long sleep.

The hedgehog walked along the hole, right to the middle, then curled up with a tired and happy grunt.

But not for long.

Scrunch, scrunch, scrunch, scrunch!

The hedgehog knew what that noise was: footsteps on the gravel. Then a voice said, "Ah, this must be the bit he wanted me to take away," and the next second the hedgehog found himself shot out of the end of the pipe and on to the ground, as a man picked up the pipe, put it under his arm and walked away.

The hedgehog was shaken but not really hurt. He picked himself up and looked around. "Where can I sleep? Oh, where can I sleep?" he said, as he began to shuffle here and there again. Then he saw a small square stone house – it was the coal bunker. The door was not quite shut. The hedgehog squeezed under it and looked about him. It was dark and warm and quite empty. Perhaps this was just the right place for a long, long sleep. He went to a corner and curled up with a tired and happy grunt.

But not for long.

Scrunch, scrunch, scrunch, scrunch!

More footsteps! Then the roof of the small, square, stone house was lifted, and down fell great black rocks. The noise was like thunder

and the poor hedgehog was nearly frightened out of his wits. When the house was full of black rocks, the roof was put back on and the footsteps went away. The hedgehog began to push and wriggle his way to the door. It took him a long time and a lot of pushing and squeezing. But at last he was outside and free, though rather dirty.

"Where can I sleep? Oh, where can I sleep?" he said, as he began to shuffle here and there again.

Then he noticed that there, underneath the shed, was a space just small enough for a hedgehog to squeeze into. Perhaps here at last was the right place for a long, long sleep.

So he crawled under the shed and shuffled about here and there until he found a pile of

leaves. Then he burrowed under them and curled up with a happy, tired grunt.

"At last!" he thought. "Somewhere safe and warm for a long, long sleep."

And there he stayed, snoring gently, right through the winter.

*   *   *

How many other animals can you think of that might live in someone's garden? In the big parks in London you might find a hedgehog, but today you would not find one on London bridge, as somebody did in this old rhyme:

As I went over London Bridge
I met Mr Rusticap;
Pins and needles on his back,
A-going to Thorney Fair.

Moonshine

HELEN DU FEU

Have you ever looked out on a moon-lit night
and seen how shiny and silvery things look?
Fishermen often go out at night, and sometimes they catch some strange "fish".

We are fishermen three,
Out we go to sea,
Big Jack, David and me

sang Grandfather Tom one dark night when
the three of them set out to sea to go fishing.
The boat was very old. It often leaked, then
the water came in, and Grandfather Tom had
to bail it out with a bucket.

The sail was torn and frayed, and the
fishing nets had holes in them.

So quite often the fish escaped and swam
away and the three fishermen had nothing to
eat for breakfast when they came home.

But tonight was different. As soon as they
had sailed away from the shore the sea became very calm. The wind died down and the
moon and the stars came out.

When they were far out to sea – so far out they couldn't see the land any more – they got ready to cast their nets.

Grandfather Tom threw his net up high, high into the sky. It was so high that he caught a sharp, silver star. He hauled in the net and put the star in the boat.

Then Big Jack threw his net out far, far across the water. He brought back crisp white foam, and put it in the boat.

Young David dropped his net over the side of the boat, deep, so deep that it came back with a silver cobweb.

Grandfather Tom wondered what he could do with his silver star.

Big Jack wondered what he could do with his crisp white foam.

Young David wondered what he could do with his silver cobweb.

So the fishermen turned the boat around and headed for home. As they went Grandfather Tom sang:

We are fishermen three,
Back we come from the sea,
Big Jack, David and me!

When they got near their village it was

nearly morning and getting light. They had another look at the things they'd caught.

Grandfather Tom looked at his star and saw that really it was a piece of metal.

Big Jack looked at his crisp white foam and saw it was really a white handkerchief.

Young David looked at his silver cobweb and saw it was really a long piece of rope.

David said, "I can mend the nets with this rope."

Big Jack said, "I can mend the sail with this white handkerchief."

And Grandfather Tom said, "I can mend the leaks in the boat with this metal."

And the next time the three fishermen put to sea, the boat looked almost new again. And all because of Moonshine!

*   *   *

One, two three four five,
Once I caught a fish alive
Six, seven, eight nine ten,
Then I let him go again.
Why did you let him go?
Because he bit my finger so.
Which finger did he bite?
This little finger on the right!

Have you heard of a leprechaun? They are supposed to be the shoemakers to the little people of Ireland. This is an old story about a leprechaun called

The Leprechaun's Gold

FELICITY HAYES McCOY

A long time ago, before the world had become noisy and rushed, it was easier to find the little people than it is now. But even then they were hard to find, they were harder to catch and they were hardest of all to hold.

In Ireland, on a still, hot summer's day, if you were very lucky you might hear the tap, tap, tap of a leprechaun's hammer. Leprechauns were quick and clever and everybody knew how rich they were. It was said that if you could catch a leprechaun and hold him tight in your hand you could make him tell you where his pot of gold was hidden. But you'd have to be very quick indeed to catch and hold him, for leprechauns are full of tricks.

Once there was a boy whose name was Michael. He lived with his mother in a little house on the edge of a bog in the middle of Ireland.

One still, hot day, in the height of summer, Michael set out early one morning to walk to school. As he trudged along the dusty road, singing to himself, he thought he heard a strange sound. So Michael stopped singing. And he listened. And, sure enough, he *had* heard a sound. It was the tap, tap, tap of a tiny hammer. It seemed to come from behind a big rock that stood by the side of the road.

So Michael crept up to the rock and peered around it. And what do you think he saw? He saw a little man sitting on the ground with a shoe in his hand. He was hammering a tiny

silver nail with a tiny golden hammer. He was dressed in scarlet and green with jewelled buckles on his little shoes. His long white beard was tucked into his leather apron, and he was humming under his breath as he worked. It was a leprechaun.

Michael didn't stop to think. Quick as a flash, he reached round the rock and caught the leprechaun up in his two hands.

"Now I have you," said Michael, "and I won't take my eye off you or let you go till you tell me where you've hidden your pot of gold."

"Ara, Michael, put me down, you have squeezed me in two," said the leprechaun. "Of course I'll tell you where to find the gold. Why wouldn't I? I'm a reasonable man. Just set me down on the ground and let me get my breath first."

"I will not," said Michael. "I've heard all about you fellows. I won't take my two hands off you till you tell me where the gold is."

"You're a desperate man," said the Leprechaun. "All right so, I'll tell you where it is. Do you see all the thorn bushes growing on that hill?" And he pointed towards the horizon.

"I do," said Michael.

"Well there's a pot of gold buried under one of them," said he. "It's buried deep, so you'll be needing a spade to dig it up with. You can carry me there if you like," said the leprechaun, "and I'll show you which bush it is."

So Michael carried the leprechaun carefully in both hands, and set off. At last they reached the foot of the hill, where the thorn bushes were growing thickly. When they were half-way up the leprechaun pointed to one of them.

"That's the one you want Michael," he said. "Will you know it again do you think?"

"I will," said Michael, "because I'll tie my red handkerchief to it as a marker. Now, listen here to me, you," he said, "I'll not let you go until you promise me that you won't touch this handkerchief while I'm gone."

"I'll promise you that all right," said the leprechaun. "Why shouldn't I? And now I'd be glad if you'd let me go in peace, Michael. I'm a peaceable man, so I am."

So Michael opened his two hands and quick as a flash the leprechaun sprang away into the bushes and disappeared.

It didn't take long for Michael to rush away to his mother's house to find a spade. Then, with the spade on his shoulder, he came panting back down the road to the hill where the thorn bushes were.

And what do you think he found when he got there?

His red handkerchief was still there, tied to the thorn bush as a marker. But if it was, it wasn't much use to him. For while Michael was gone the leprechaun had tied a red handkerchief to *every* thorn bush that grew on the hillside – and there were hundreds and

hundreds and hundreds of them.

Poor Michael! It would have taken a year's digging to dig under every thorn bush. So what was he to do?

He put his spade back on his shoulder and he trudged back down the hill again.

And as he went he could hear a strange sound. It was the sound of the leprechaun breaking his heart laughing on the hillside.

*   *   *

What's in here?
Gold and money.

Where's my share of it?
The mousie ran away from it.

Where's the mousie?
In his housie.

Where's the housie?
In the wood.

Where's the wood?
The fire burnt it.

Where's the fire?
The water quenched it.

124

Where's the water?
The brown bull drank it.

Where's the brown bull?
On Burnie's Hill.

Where's Burnie's Hill?
All dressed in snow.

Where's the snow?
The sun melted it.

Where's the sun?
High, high in the sky!

Acknowledgements

Our thanks are due to writers who have given us permission to reprint copyright material and to the following:

Marcia Armitage for *I tried on a hat*; Ruth Craft for *Mrs Slam-Bang*; André Deutsch Ltd. for *I'm just going out for a moment* by Michael Rosen; Julia Donaldson for *Pull a funny face*; David Higham Associates Ltd. for *King's Cross* by Eleanor Farjeon; Patrick Smythe for *I'm a humpity camel*.

A bit of jungle in the street is by Esther Valck George; *A piper in the streets today* is by Seumas O'Sullivan; *Frodge Dobbulum* is by W. B. Rands.

In the middle of my back by Judy Whitfield is © British Broadcasting Corporation

The remainder of the verses are from traditional sources.